Dedicated to Marjane Wood

First Red Wagon Books edition 1996

Red Wagon Books is a registered trademark of Harcourt Brace & Company.

Library of Congress Cataloging-in-Publication Data
Wood. Don 1945
Piggies/Don and Audrey Wood; illustrated by Don Wood.
p. cm.
Summary: Ten little piggies dance on a young child's fingers and toes
before finally going to sleep.
ISBN 0-15-256341-5
ISBN 0-15-200217-0 (pbk.)
ISBN 0-15-201063-7 (miniature edition)
[1. Bedtime — Fiction. 2. Games — Fiction. 3. Pigs — Fiction.]
I. Wood, Audrey. II. Title.
PZ7.W8473P1 [E]—dc20 89-24598
C E G H F D

The original paintings in this book were done in oil on Bristol board.
The text type was set in Goudy Catalogue.
The display type was set in Caxton Book.
Color separations were made by Bright Arts, Ltd., Singapore
Printed and bound by RR Donnelley & Sons Company, Reynosa, Mexico
Production supervision by Warren Wallerstein and Ginger Boyer

Piggies

WRITTEN BY
DON AND AUDREY WOOD

ILLUSTRATED BY
DON WOOD

Red Wagon Books
Harcourt Brace & Company
SAN DIEGO   NEW YORK   LONDON

I've got two

fat little piggies,

two smart

little piggies,

two   long

little piggies,

two silly

little piggies,

and two wee

little piggies.

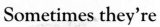

Sometimes they're

hot little piggies,

and sometimes they're

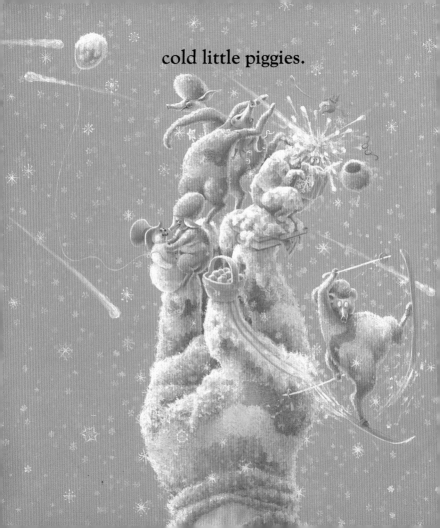

cold little piggies.

Sometimes they're

clean little piggies,

and sometimes they're

dirty little piggies.

Sometimes they're

good little piggies,

but not at bedtime. That's when

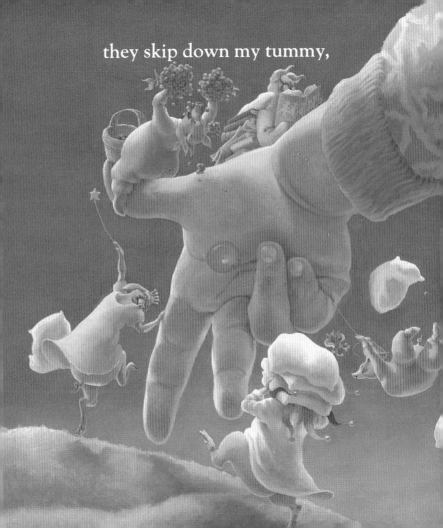

they skip down my tummy,

dance on my toes,

then run away and hide.

So . . .

…I put them together, all in a row,

for two fat kisses,

two smart kisses,

two long kisses,

two silly kisses,

and two wee kisses goodnight.